I Love Dad

To my friend Mark
– *JA*

SIMON AND SCHUSTER
First published in Great Britain in 2015 by Simon and Schuster UK Ltd
1st Floor, 222 Gray's Inn Road, London WC1X 8HB
A CBS Company

Text copyright © 2015 J.M. Walsh
Illustrations copyright © 2015 Giuditta Gaviraghi

ISBN: 978-0-85707-584-0 (PB)
ISBN: 978-1-4711-2362-7 (eBook)
Printed in China
2 4 6 8 10 9 7 5 3 1

I Love Dad

J.M. Walsh & Judi Abbot

SIMON AND SCHUSTER
London New York Sydney Toronto New Delhi

Nobody in the morning
yawns so big as **Dad**.

Nobody's snores so awesome.

Nobody's kisses are so bristly
nobody's stubble so
double-itchy
but

who else could be so tickly,
trick so quickly?

No one else makes breakfast into a festival.
Dad throws the best a.m. party ever.

I'd never thought juice and cereal
really special.

Who'd have guessed it?

Who else gives me a feeling
of being tall as
the ceiling?
Better go outside
where . . .

nobody's shoulders could be higher,
so near the sky for such
a bumpy ride.

Nobody's arms are
such an aeroplane,

nobody's foot a swing,

no one's knees such
a queasy trampoline.

Now, says **Dad**, let's get out the bikes,
pump up the tyres until we burst for air!
A dab of grease,
some oil-squirts here
and there.
No one was ever such a fixer-upper.
Then . . .

Dad on wheels!
Dad in the saddle
cycles faster than a bike'll pedal . . .

till we're
tired and then we
freewheel
downhill to home.

But, if it rains,
who else wakes up parades of toys
and makes them walk and speak?
Who . . .

gets out boards and cards
and chases pieces round?
A tiddlywink to finish first
and a card house
to tumble down.
Then . . .

Cooking with **Dad's** a laugh,
a lark, not half
a spoonful wasted. No!
We get a bellyful
of just-another-taste.

Who loves to eat
sausages, spaghetti, pizza?

But who always makesh shure
I BRUSH MY TEESH?

Who can make
a bedtime story so fantastic,
a lion's roar so drastic,
   a plastic man's
      kung-fu kick
         so slick?

And when the clock ticks round
to time for sleep,
in dreams I know
tomorrow will be full
of things to do
with **Dad**
again.